BENJI FRANKLIN

KID ZILLIONAIRE

INVESTING WELL

(IN SUPERSONIC SPACESHIPS!)

written by
Raymond Bean

illustrated by
Matthew Vimislik

Contents

Introduction

My name's Benji Franklin! After inventing a best-selling computer app that helps people come up with creative and time-saving excuses, I became the world's youngest and, well, only ZILLIONAIRE!

But I quickly discovered that life wasn't all about money. I've decided to use my newly found wealth for the greater good – such as saving the world from cloned killer dinosaurs, building super-powered rocket ships and launching a solid gold submarine. Or two!

CHAPTER 1
Three billion is bonkers

Dad and I were out in the workshop, looking at a robot he'd designed. It was a pretty cool idea, and he'd put a lot of time into it. As the robot moved, it created friction. The friction was used to create electricity, and the electricity was then used to continue powering the robot. You didn't have to plug it in or use batteries. It just went on its own. He'd built it out of parts from an old computer, a metal rubbish bin and a pair of roller skates.

I was so focused on the robot that I hardly noticed the sound of a helicopter landing in the field behind the workshop. I might not have noticed it at all if it weren't for all the dust it kicked up. Dust swirled through the doorway like a sandstorm. I was glad I was wearing a welding mask

Dad and I walked out of the workshop without a word and looked at the helicopter coming to rest in the field. A year ago, I would have been shocked to see a helicopter approaching our land, but my life had become pretty exciting lately. I wasn't really that surprised.

The blades slowed down and three men got out. They all wore business suits. Two of the men were dressed in black and wore black sunglasses. It looked like they were in the Secret Service or something.

The two men dressed in black stayed close to the other man as he walked towards Dad and me. It was like a scene from an action film, but if it had been an action film, he would have been walking in slow motion.

The blades on the helicopter had completely stopped by the time he reached us.

"I'm looking for Benji Franklin," he said.

"I had a feeling you'd say that," my dad said, pulling off his welding mask.

"I'm Benji Franklin," I said, leaving mine on.

"I can't believe you're really a kid," he said. He was pretty short, much shorter than Dad. He had a long white beard that didn't seem to match his business suit.

"I had a feeling you'd say that, too," Dad said.

"Is there somewhere we can talk that's more private?" he asked.

I looked around. There wasn't another person in sight. The only other people were the men in black suits.

"Don't you trust your buddies over there?" I asked.

"I don't know who to trust these days," he said.

Dad waved for him to follow and walked back towards the workshop. The workshop and my house sit on land that has been in our family for generations. Most people would take one look at it and think it was a scrapyard, but to me it was like buried treasure. Old car parts, pieces of boats and aeroplanes, and mysterious pieces of large equipment poked out from long, overgrown grass.

There were half-finished projects all over the workshop. Dad and I had been working, so it was even more of a mess than usual. I could tell Dad was trying to find something clean for the man to sit on but couldn't.

"I won't take up too much of your time. My name is Mark Crow," the man said, clearly realizing there was nowhere for him to sit. "I have a problem that I'd like solved as quietly as possible, and I'm told Benji may be the right person for the job."

I sat on one of the boxes a delivery man had brought in earlier that morning. Mr Crow sat on the one next to me. As I got comfortable, I realized I didn't know what was in the boxes, but they had been sent from my school. They were pretty big. It made me wonder what was inside.

"What's the problem?" I asked.

"Benji has just finished a job," Dad said before Mr Crow could reply. "He has a tremendous amount of school work to complete, and I don't think that he'll have the time for anything else."

I shook my head to indicate that I disagreed. Although I had just returned from a job, I was ready to get back to work.

"What's the problem?" I asked Mr Crow again.

"It's complicated," he said.

"Complicated is sort of my thing."

"I represent a very small, but powerful, group of business people," he explained. "Recently we've all been victims of the same crime."

"What kind of crime?" I asked.

I was feeling more like a superhero than ever. I imagined my dad as my loyal sidekick. He's a little old to be a sidekick, but what can you do?

"Benji is more of a scientist than a detective," Dad said.

"I've been known to dabble in a little detective work from time to time," I said, embracing my inner superhero.

"A robbery," he said, glancing over his shoulder.

"Where did the robbery take place?" I asked. "Also, you do know that there's no one out here watching us, right?"

"You can never be too careful. And to answer your question about the location of the robbery, that's the complicated part. It wasn't one robbery. It was several large robberies that happened all at once. They're probably taking place right now."

"I don't understand," Dad said.

"We own some of the largest companies in the world. We own fast-food chains, clothing companies, sportswear shops, car companies – you name it, and we probably own it," he said.

"Burger Slam?" I asked.

"We own it."

"Game Revolution?" I asked.

"We own that, too, and most of the companies that make the games they sell."

"Jumbo's Supermarket?" I asked.

"We own it and most of the companies that supply the goods to the shops. As I said, if you've heard of it, one of us probably owns it. If you haven't heard of it, we probably own it. That's what makes what's happened so unbelievable."

"I still don't really understand," I said.

"Our digital transactions, when someone uses a credit card, are being hijacked."

"When you say hijacked..." Dad asked.

"I mean that the charges are going through – customers are paying using their credit cards – but the money doesn't go into our accounts. It disappears," said Mr Crow.

"How much money have you lost?" I asked.

"So far, about three billion."

"You mean million?" I asked.

"No, you heard me correctly. We've lost about three billion dollars," he groaned.

If I had had long hair, it would have blown back. "Billion with a 'b', like bat?" I asked.

"Billion with a 'b' like bananas," he said.

"WOW! That's, well … bonkers!" I joked.

"No kidding. It's a nightmare! We're not sure what to do. We can't stop taking credit cards or our customers will think something is wrong."

"But something is wrong," I pointed out.

"Yes, but they can't know that. We have to conduct business as usual, but we're losing a huge amount of money in the process."

"You should really talk to the police or the FBI," Dad pointed out.

"We would like to keep this as quiet as possible. If we involve the authorities, the story will be all over the news, and people might stop using our shops and services. We want this fixed quickly and quietly. We can't have people thinking it's not safe to do business with us."

"But it's not safe," I said.

"That's why I'm here talking to you. I need that fixed, and I need it fixed as quickly as possible."

"I'll have to talk to Benji's mother and his headmistress about this before he can commit to helping you," Dad said.

"I completely understand, but we'll need to know in the next twenty-four hours. Every second that passes could be more money lost. Also, if news of this spreads, we'll have a major panic on our hands. So you mustn't tell anyone."

CHAPTER 2
Merci

"There's no way you can take on another job," Mum said that night at dinner.

"I know I've been really busy lately," I pleaded, "but this is an amazing mission."

"You mean 'job', Benji. You get so caught up in them that they really become full-time jobs."

"Remember, he likes to think of himself as a superhero. So he prefers it if we call them missions," Dad said.

I nodded. He was right. I'd gone from being a kid that invented a successful app to someone who secretly solved the world's problems. Why shouldn't they be called missions? Calling them jobs sounded too much like work – it just didn't feel right.

"How about we call them adventures?" Dad suggested.

"It really doesn't matter what we call them," Mum said. "Benji needs to take a break for a while."

"Sir Robert thinks I should stop going to school for a while and focus on my missions and creating new apps," I explained.

Sir Robert had said this more than once, and I knew that he'd mentioned it to Mum and Dad.

"Sir Robert is not your mother," said Mum.

"He is a billionaire who's travelled the world." I said, knowing I was testing my mum's patience.

"And as much as he's helped you, I'm beginning to wonder if he has your best interests at heart. But we're not talking about him right now. We're talking about you, and you need to experience a normal childhood and a normal education."

"But Benji has a spaceship, a submarine and more money than we can keep track of," Dad added.

"I think the idea of a 'normal childhood' may be a stretch at this point."

"I realize that," Mum said, "but I want him to have as normal a childhood as he can. I accept that he's already wildly successful at a very young age, but that doesn't mean he should stop learning and stop living like a normal child."

"You always say that I should use my knowledge for the greater good, right?" I asked.

"Yes," she said.

"Well, the man that came here today said there are thousands of people who have been robbed. They need my help."

"That sounds like a job for the police."

"He wants it done quietly," Dad interrupted.

"Isn't there anyone else who can solve these problems? Why are all these successful people always coming to you to save the day?" Mum asked.

"You know the answer to that question," I said.

"A superhero, eh?" she asked giving a slight smile.

"I'm not like other kids, Mum."

"I realized that when you taught yourself French at nursery," she said.

"It does sound like an interesting opportunity," Dad added. Dad was funny. I could tell he was just as excited as me, or even more, but he tried not to show it in front of Mum.

"If you can work out a way to solve this," she paused, "mission, without missing any school, I'll give you my permission."

"*Merci*," I said, using my French.

"You're welcome," she said, giving me a smile. "School comes first."

"Agreed," I said.

Of course, I had no idea how I was going to solve these mysterious robberies without missing any school. School was very demanding, and I'd missed a lot of it lately. I knew I had a lot of school work piling up, but I didn't know what was due and when. I'd have to get my mind back onto my books and get caught up if Mum was ever going to let me take on this mission.

CHAPTER 3

I take your point, but I don't like it

In the morning, my driver picked me up earlier than usual. It was my first day back at school after my last mission, and I wanted to get on top of things.

"How was your last mission, sir?" Mr Kensington, my driver, asked.

"It was a total adventure," I said. "I got to use my submarine, and I was attacked by a giant squid. It was pretty awesome."

"A giant squid! Wow! You're leading an exciting life these days," he said. "Were you paid well?"

"A few million dollars, and I'm now a part-owner of a deep-sea gold mine."

"Not bad for a week's work," Kensington said.

"Not bad at all!" I agreed.

He stopped the car in front of the school. "Let's hope your good luck holds up when you meet with your headmistress." I thanked him and walked into school. I went straight to the headmistress's office.

She was on the phone, but hung up when she saw me coming. "Benji Franklin," she said, "how nice of you to pop in and say hello."

The tone of her voice made it sound as though she was upset with me, which was strange because she was usually very cool.

"Is something wrong?" I asked.

"No, but you missed more school than I expected on your last adventure. I spoke to your mother about it, and we agree that you should take a break from missing school for a while."

"I know," I said. "We already talked about it at home." I realized there was no point in trying to get out of more school or to explain why I needed a few more days to work on the new mission. "I think you're probably right," I said.

"Good. You're going to need all of your attention on school work in order to catch up on everything you've missed."

I thought I'd missed a few projects, but it couldn't be too bad. She logged onto her computer and made a face. "Oh my. You have several projects that are overdue."

"That can't be right. You said you were going to send me any work to complete while I was away. I haven't been sent anything."

"I had asked Cindy to keep track of your work and pass things on to you as she's in all of your lessons," the headmistress explained.

"She didn't email me anything while I was away," I said. It made sense, too, because Cindy was always having a go at me about everything. She probably didn't send them on purpose just so I'd get into trouble.

"That's odd. Why don't you track her down and see if she'll tell you what you've missed."

I wasn't looking forward to seeing Cindy. She always had a go at me about being out of school. She did help me a little bit with my last mission, which was a nice surprise, but now it seemed as though we were right back to her giving me a hard time.

I walked out of Mrs Petty's office and down to my secret office in the storage cupboard. I held my hand up to the word *storage* on the door and it unlocked. I glanced over my shoulder to make sure no one was looking and slipped in.

I knew Cindy had been in my office while I was away, but I still couldn't work out how she'd done it. The only way to get in was to scan your hand over the sign and, as far as I knew, no one else had the same fingerprints as me!

I sat at my desk and realized straight away that my computer and all my screens were gone. An ancient-looking computer, like the ones in the classrooms, sat on the desk. I felt as though I was in some kind of a time warp. I hadn't used a computer that old since I was a baby. The computer was probably older than me! I tried to log in, but I was denied access.

Just then I heard the door open and close. From behind the pile of boxes in front of my desk, Cindy appeared. "Hello, welcome back," she said.

"How'd you get in here? Where's my computer?" I asked.

"Didn't your mother ever teach you to say hello to someone when they say hello to you?"

"Of course she did," I said, "but right now I would like to know where my computers are."

"Mrs Petty gave me permission to remove them. I sent them back to your house."

That must have been the boxes that were delivered the day before. "Why would she do that?"

"She realized, after I pointed it out, that it wasn't fair for you to have access to the latest technology when the rest of the pupils use the oldest computers known to humans."

"But she agreed to let me use this office," I said.

"That's true, and I tried to convince her that it was unfair and that you should lose that privilege, but she said she had worked out some sort of agreement with you and that man Sir Robert."

She was right. Sir Robert had convinced Mrs Petty that if my parents were going to make me continue to go to school like a normal kid, I should have a secret office where I could work on my missions in peace. Now Cindy was trying to take that away.

"Why do you care if I have a secret office?"

"Because it's not fair. I'm the head of the Committee for Fairness and Equality for our school, and I couldn't sit by while something like this was going on that is unfair for all the pupils."

"But how am I supposed to get anything done now?" I asked. "These computers look like they came over on the Mayflower."

"Don't be ridiculous," she said. "There weren't computers when the Mayflower sailed."

I didn't have time to explain to Cindy that I was only joking because the first bell rang.

"We'll have to find some time later today to talk about all the school work you've missed," she said.

"How come you didn't send me my projects? I could have worked on them while I was away."

"I tried emailing you on the computers from school, but the connection is very unreliable. Most of the time the emails don't go through."

"Why didn't you just send stuff from your home computer or tell me when we talked on the phone?"

"Mrs Petty asked me to email you the projects from school. That's what I did. I tried from school several times, and the technology failed. That's not my fault," Cindy said.

I didn't want to spend another moment arguing with Cindy, so I slipped out into the corridor and made my way to my first lesson.

As soon as I walked through the door, my Maths teacher handed me a folder full of work that was due by the end of the week. The same thing happened in English, History and Science.

I went to Mrs Petty's office at the end of the day, dropped all the work on her desk and fell into the chair. She looked at me and smiled. It was a bit strange, because I didn't feel like smiling at all, and she had a huge grin on her face.

"It looks like you have some work ahead of you this week," she said.

"I do, and I'll get it done," I explained. "But I don't understand why Cindy or my teachers couldn't have emailed everything I needed."

"The system isn't very reliable when it comes to emails and the internet," said Mrs Petty. "Cindy tried, but her emails must not have gone through."

"Don't you think that's a problem?" I asked. "Everything takes place online these days. The school should really have better computers."

"You're right, but our system is very out-of-date."

"What about my office? How come Cindy snuck in and removed all of my technology?"

"Don't ask me how she got in. I don't even have access to that space, and I'm the headmistress. However, it did seem like the only fair thing to do. You can use the office,

33

of course, as we agreed. But I feel it's not fair to the other students if you're allowed access to better equipment."

"But those were my computers," I reminded her. "I paid for them. I wasn't using up any of the school's resources."

"True," Mrs Petty agreed. "But unless you plan on buying new computers for the entire school, I'm afraid you'll have to use the same old computers as everyone else when you're here."

I could buy new computers for everyone in the district if I wanted to, but it wasn't my job to supply computers for schools.

"As much as I'd like to help the school," I said, "It's not fair for me to have to buy them for everyone."

"Then you'll understand why it's not fair for you to have the very best, while the rest of the pupils here have to work with old computers."

I understood her point, but I still didn't like it.

CHAPTER 4

Name your price

That night, Mum, Dad and I were at the farm checking up on the livestock when Mr Crow landed his helicopter on one of the old runways. The farm had been an old airport before we converted it to a farm.

The same two Secret-Service–looking men from the other day were with him. He introduced himself to Mum and invited us all to go for a ride. He said he wanted to show us something that might help us to make our decision. I didn't tell him that Mum had already decided to give me permission to take on his mission.

"It's happened again," he said over the headphones once we were in the air.

"What's happened exactly?" Mum asked.

"The majority of the money that exchanged hands today across the entire country for my group's businesses has vanished. One moment it was there and the next – POOF – it was all gone. We're talking about almost every transaction from our shops, websites, fast-food restaurants and car dealerships. It's a major situation, and we can't keep it quiet much longer. And when word gets out about this, we're all in big trouble. Worse still, if our businesses suffer, the people that work in them may lose their jobs."

"Can't you simply track the money?" Dad asked.

"We're talking about electronic money, Mr Franklin," Mr Crow explained. "It's not like notes that we can put fingerprint powder on or track the numbers on the notes or anything like that. This money is digital. It's gone somewhere in cyberspace, but we don't know where 'somewhere' is."

My phone vibrated. It was Sir Robert.

"Please don't breathe a word of this to anyone else," Mr Crow pleaded.

"It's just Sir Robert. He's basically my partner," I said.

"No disrespect, but I don't want Robert knowing about what's happened," he said.

"You know Sir Robert?" I asked.

"Yes," Mr Crow replied, "and I don't want him to know what's happened or that you're helping me. He's one of my competitors. I don't want him to have the satisfaction of knowing I'm being hacked. For all I know, it's him."

"Please put your phone away, Mr Franklin," one of the men in black said.

I clicked to ignore the call and felt a bit strange about it. Sir Robert had always been my mentor and someone I talked to about all of my missions. It would be odd working without him.

"I realize that Sir Robert and you have a history

of working together, but if you take this job, you mustn't breathe a word of it to him. Do you think you can do that?"

I looked at Mum and Dad. "I can." I was really excited about the mission, but I hadn't expected to have to hide it from Sir Robert.

I felt myself slip off into a bit of a daydream. There were so many things on my mind – the school work I'd missed, the missing money, Sir Robert. It all swirled in my head.

"Do you have any ideas about how to work out what's going on?" Mum asked. She knew me so well. Sometimes I slip into a bit of a haze, and then the idea comes to me. It's sort of like a waking dream.

"I do," I said. I had the beginnings of a plan forming.

"Your reputation for fast work is accurate," Mr Crow said.

"It's not fully formed yet," I explained, "but I can see a solution to your problem. I think we can catch the hacker and get your businesses back to normal, but it's not going to be cheap."

This was always one of my favourite parts of the mission. It was interesting to see how people reacted to the news that solving their problem might be done quickly but would be very expensive.

"If you can solve this problem, you can name your price," he said. That was the answer I'd been hoping for.

"Fantastic," I said. "Do you have any companies that sell computers?"

"Of course," Mr Crow replied. "We own the three biggest computer companies in the country."

"I'm going to need a lot of computers," I said.

"How many?" he asked.

"About five hundred to start, but I'll need a lot more when the job is finished."

"That doesn't seem like a problem," he said.

"I'll need you to deliver them to my school first thing tomorrow morning."

"I'll make the call the moment we're back on the ground," he said.

CHAPTER 5
Special delivery

I woke up before sunrise the next morning. I was really excited about getting to work. I looked out of my window and saw that the light in the workshop was already on, so I got dressed and went downstairs.

"What are you doing up already?" Dad asked.

"I'm excited about getting to work." I couldn't wait to see Mrs Petty's face when those computers started rolling in. "What are you doing up so early?"

"I had a breakthrough with my robot last night. I haven't been to bed yet," Dad said. Dad sometimes got so caught up in his work that he worked through the night.

I felt my phone buzz in my pocket. It was Sir Robert calling. "I should answer this," I said.

"Hello, dear boy," Sir Robert said. His face was very close to the screen on his phone.

"Hi, Sir Robert."

"How are you, Benji? I haven't heard from you since you returned from your last trip."

"I know," I said. "I've been busy getting on with my school work. I got back to a pretty huge pile of it."

"Tell your headmistress that you're busy with things far more important than reports and homework. The world is your classroom now."

"Tell that to my mum," I said. "She doesn't even want me taking on any new missions."

"She wants you to be like other children. I understand that. I just don't feel school should be holding you back from your calling in life. Have you had any job offers since your last mission? Several of my business associates have asked for your contact information. Your services are very much in demand."

"Nothing too exciting. Like I said, Mum won't let me take off any more time from school, so I can't do much." I felt bad about not telling him the truth, but I had promised Mr Crow.

Later that morning, during my second lesson, I noticed three black vans pull up in front of the school. Through the window I watched as one of the drivers walked up to the front of the school and went inside. I waited for the announcement that I was

sure was going to come over the PA system as soon as Mrs Petty learned what was in the vans.

I looked at the clock. The announcement would come any second. I counted down in my mind. Five, four, three, two, one… It came right on cue: "Excuse the interruption. Would Benji Franklin report to the main office, please? Benji Franklin to the main office."

The kids in the classroom all looked at me like I was in trouble, but I just smiled. I couldn't wait to see the look on Mrs Petty's face. I strolled out of the classroom and made my way slowly to the office.

I walked in and Mrs Petty said, "May I speak to you in my office, please, Benji?"

"Of course," I said. The driver sat in the chair that kids sit in when they're in trouble and waiting for the headmistress.

We walked in, and she closed the door behind us.

"What's going on?" she asked once the door was completely closed.

"You said I could have my computers back if I updated the computers for the school. I worked out a way to make that happen," I explained.

"Benji, as generous and considerate as that may be, you can't simply make a decision like this without asking me first."

"I thought we talked about it yesterday," I said.

"Well, I didn't expect you to go out and find a way to provide new computers for the entire school the next day," Mrs Petty replied.

"Well, I did," I said. "It's the way I roll.

"It's not that simple, Benji," she said. "We are one school in a very large school district. I can't accept new computers for this school if the other schools don't have the same opportunity."

I knew she would say that and had already agreed with Mr Crow that I could get more computers if I needed them.

"If you allow for these computers to be installed today, I promise you that I'll get new computers for the entire school district when my mission is over," I said. Then I realized I was in a position to negotiate. "But I'd like something in return."

"I'm listening," she said.

"Give me a week off, but at school. I have a new mission, and it's going to need all of my attention. I can't be distracted by reports, late homework or going to lessons. I also need you to forget about the projects that I've missed."

"This is highly irregular. Pupils don't generally come into the headmistress's office and negotiate their way out of missed deadlines and going to lessons."

"But they also don't offer to supply new computers for the school district. I'm saving the district millions, and helping the school at the same time."

"You have a good point," she said. "I'll give you a week to complete your new mission. If at the end of the week you supply new computers for the entire district, I'll tell your teachers to forget about your missed projects."

"You have yourself a deal," I said. "You also have new computers for the school."

"I've never had a pupil quite like you, Benji Franklin," said Mrs Petty.

I wasn't sure if she meant that as a compliment or if she was criticizing me, but I had an opportunity to solve the robberies, avoid my missing work and keep my promise to Mum that I wouldn't miss any time from school.

"One more thing," I said.

"I'm afraid to ask," she said.

Then I said something that I thought would knock her off her chair. "I'd like Cindy to be my partner on this mission."

CHAPTER 6
Invisible data

Later that night, Dad and I decided we should head up into space. We needed to get a better look at the satellites orbiting Earth to have a better understanding of how they worked. We climbed into the cockpit, and my spaceship's computer said, "Good evening, Mr Franklin and Mr Franklin."

"Good evening, Saunders," I said.

Saunders opened the roof of the building. The stars shined brightly. We lifted off slowly, rising up like a helicopter, hovering above the hangar. Once we were high enough, and had cleared the building, I hit the booster rockets, and we were off like a shot. Within minutes, we were out of Earth's atmosphere.

I turned on the GPS and asked Saunders to show

us all the satellites in orbit. Then I asked Saunders to show me all the satellites owned by Mr Crow's companies.

Saunders was a robot, I understood that, but I sort of thought of him as a person, too. He seemed so human that it was hard to remember that he was simply a complex computer program.

"I'm displaying all the known satellites orbiting Earth in blue. I've highlighted the ones owned by the Crow Corporation and its companies in green.

"Thank you," I said.

"You do not have to thank me, sir," Saunders said.

"It's just a computer," Dad said.

"Yes, but he's extraordinarily smart." As I said the words, I felt something about the mission fall into place. The transactions were made using computers. People slid their credit cards through the computers at the shop and after that every other step was completed by a computer.

The reason why Mr Crow and his companies couldn't work out who was stealing their money was because the person stealing their money wasn't a person at all. It was probably a computer that was programmed to steal and then cover its tracks.

Luckily for me, I had just had five hundred new computers installed at school. All I had to do now was program them to work together, and we may just be able to catch the thief.

"Benji, are you okay?" Dad asked. "You haven't said anything for a while."

I had slipped off into a daydream. It felt as though only a few seconds had passed. "I'm fine," I said. "Just thinking."

"We're approaching the first satellite," he said.

I looked out of the window of the spaceship. The satellite was like a floating tube with mirrors and long, flat panels on either side. The panels were solar panels, tilted towards the sun for energy to power the satellite.

We zoomed ahead to the next satellite. It looked a lot like the first one, but it was much larger. The most interesting thing about seeing the satellites up close in space was that you couldn't see the data. It's completely invisible. Dad and I zipped from satellite to satellite. If you didn't know each one was transmitting loads of data back and forth to Earth, you'd think it was just a floating piece of metal.

There had to be a way to follow the data and track where it went and how it moved. For that, I realized, I'd need a few satellites of my own.

Dad and I had made and launched satellites ourselves in the past. We even had one orbiting Earth looking for dangerous asteroids. The ones we had made, though, were not nearly as advanced as I needed for this mission. I needed a few satellites that could work faster than the satellites being robbed. And I needed them right away.

CHAPTER 7

Welcome to my lair

That night I called Mr Crow while we were in space and told him we'd need a few satellites immediately in order to solve the problem.

"Benji," Mr Crow began, "I can honestly say that when I was put in touch with you I didn't really have high hopes that you'd be able to actually find a solution to my problem. I didn't think a child was capable of tackling something so enormous, but people told me to trust that you were capable of the task, and I did. Who knew there were twelve-year-olds with their own spaceships?"

"Actually, I'm the only one," I said.

"Of course you are," he said. "I will get you the satellites you need, but I'd also like to meet tomorrow morning to talk about your plan. Can you put together a price list for me so I have an idea of what I'm going to spend? I'll have to run it by my associates."

"I'll be at school tomorrow," I said. "But if you'd like to pop in, I'll be working on your mission. I'll send over exactly what I'll need and a breakdown of the costs in a few minutes."

"I'll see you tomorrow then," said Mr Crow. "Right now, I'm going to get to work on finding you those satellites. See you in the morning."

I typed up the bill for Mr Crow and emailed it to him.

Fuel for spaceship	$175,000
Satellite delivery	$200,000
Total cost for project	$4,175,000
20% consultation fee	$200,000
Total amount due	$4,375,000

*2,000 computers No charge, supplied by Mr Crow (Value $2,200,000)
*Satellite supplied by Mr Crow (Value $1,600,000)

I asked Kensington to pick me up at four o'clock the next morning.

"You're really getting a lot of school work done," he said. "I don't think I've ever seen you this committed to school."

"I made a deal with my mum and the headmistress. I agreed to not miss any school, and I agreed to solve the mission by the end of the week."

"It sounds like a lot of pressure," he said.

I suppose it was, but I didn't think of it that way. To me it was an adventure and a game all rolled up into one. I'd managed to convince Mum to let me take on the mission, and I'd convinced the headmistress to let me miss lessons all week. I had to succeed.

I was at school before Mrs Petty. I put a note on her desk to call me when she arrived and went to my office to work.

I tried to hack my way into one of Mr Crow's satellites, but it was too complex. Then I tried to access the computers at a few of his shops, but the code was too complicated to crack. I knew if I had more time I'd be able to get in without a problem, but we didn't have time. I'd have to work something out – and fast.

Before I knew it, it was seven-thirty. My phone rang, and it was Mrs Petty. "Good morning, Benji," she said. "I just arrived and saw your note. Also, there's a Mr Crow and two other gentlemen here to meet with you."

"Super! Can you and Mr Crow come down to my office?"

A few minutes later they knocked on the door. I let them in and closed the door behind them. I had set up my computers already and was busy at work.

"What is this?" Mr Crow asked.

"Good morning, Mr Crow. This is my lair."

"I should have known you'd have a lair," he said. "A secret hideout, stopping the bad guys – all you need is a cape and you'll be all set."

"You're not the first person to tell me that," I said. "I've been considering wearing a cape, but I think that may be going a little overboard."

"Just a little," Cindy said, walking in.

I didn't know how she'd made it in again! I'd closed the door behind Mrs Petty and Mr Crow. She had worked out a way to hack my security and instead of being mad about it, I was sort of curious.

"How do you do it?" I asked.

"I told you," replied Cindy, "you're not the only genius at our school."

CHAPTER 8
It's all about you

Cindy looked as though she'd woken up on the wrong side of the bed or something. I decided it was probably the wrong time to ask her more questions about how she was getting through my security.

"I know that you and I haven't exactly got along in the past," I said.

"You could say that," she said.

"But I have a new mission, and I think you can be a big help."

"Why would you want my help?" Cindy asked.

"Well," I began, "you're always having a go at me about missing school when I'm on my missions. I thought that if you helped me with one, you might understand how important they are and get off my back."

"So it's all about you? Why am I not surprised?"

"Actually," Mrs Petty said. "Benji's missions are usually about helping other people. If they weren't, I would never let him miss school. In this case, the people he's helping are the pupils of our school."

"Can I tell her what's going on?" I asked Mr Crow.

"If you think she needs to know," he said.

I explained to Cindy that Mr Crow's companies were being robbed and that I had a plan to stop it, but I needed her help.

"Why do you need my help?" she asked.

"You're the head of every committee in this school. You're used to working with large groups of people to get something done."

"I still don't understand why you need my help," she said.

"I'm launching a few satellites today that are going to capture all the digital activity at Mr Crow's businesses. I've written a program that captures the data and slows it down, but the program is too long and complicated for me to enter it on my own. I don't have time to enter the computer code by the end of the week. Also, I think that whoever is hacking Mr Crow's system has coded the computers so that other computers can't detect what's going on. To catch this cyber-criminal we're going to need eyes on the data, not just computers. This project is going to take the whole school. We'll need every pupil working on it."

Mrs Petty made a strange face, as though she was in pain.

"You can guarantee new computers for the entire district?" she asked.

"Guaranteed," I said, looking at Mr Crow. He nodded.

"I'll have to meet with the teaching staff and see if they agree to this," said Mrs Petty.

"Think of it as a team-building exercise. If we can work together as a team, we can learn so many skills that we'll need in the real world," Cindy said.

"We never discussed this," Mrs Petty said. "Teachers tell the pupils what to do, Benji. It's generally not the other way around."

Mrs Petty was quiet for a few minutes, and then she said, "What do you think, Cindy? Can you organize everyone to help to write the computer code for Mr Crow?"

"I can. And I will under one condition," she said. "I don't have to take orders from you. I'll be in charge of the kids."

"This is all highly unusual," Mr Crow said. "My associates are never going to believe I'm letting a group of school kids solve a multi-billion dollar cyber-heist. I'll give you until the end of the week, Benji."

"Are you in?" I asked Cindy.

"I'm in," she replied. "Let's get to work."

***

Mrs Petty called a meeting with all the teachers to explain that for the next few days the kids would be working on a school-wide computer project.

Cindy got to work breaking up my code for small groups. Each group would be assigned a part of the code to enter into the computer.

At nine o'clock, Mrs Petty announced that we were having an assembly. The entire school stopped working and went to the school hall. Cindy and I joined Mrs Petty on the stage.

"Good morning, pupils," she said. "I've called you together to share some very exciting news. As you all know by now, Benji Franklin is often out of school because he has been working on top-secret missions. This week, you will all get a chance to be involved in one."

The room was quiet. The kids didn't seem to know what was going on. Mrs Petty waved me over to the microphone. I'd never talked to a large group like that before and felt really nervous all of a sudden. I leaned in to the microphone, which I could hardly reach.

"Good morning. I know a lot of you secretly hate that I get to miss school a lot because of my super-cool missions, but this week you get a chance to be a part of one." The room was still quiet, and I couldn't tell what the kids were thinking. I knew I had to turn up the interest level if I was going to win them over. "Mrs Petty has agreed to cancel lessons and homework for the rest of the week!" I announced.

The room erupted. It was as if they'd won the lottery or something.

Mrs Petty made her way back to the microphone, and the room quietened down. "We're going to work together on a school-wide computer-programming project," she explained. "While we're working on the project, I have cancelled lessons and homework. Cindy Myers will divide the school into one hundred groups of ten. Each group will be responsible for entering a string of code that will be part of the larger code that will help Benji to complete his mission."

The room cheered again, and then Cindy took the microphone. "I'll email every student his or her group and the string of code to enter. Benji and I will be around if you need any help. We have only a few days to do this, so please work together and do your best. If we can complete the project successfully, we can earn computers for the whole school district."

CHAPTER 9

Invisible money

The next day, Mr Crow sent me the access codes and passwords to all of his satellites. Cindy and I helped each group at school to start working on writing code and linking everything into the new satellite. It was a massive job, but by breaking it into smaller pieces it seemed possible. Cindy was really good at organizing the groups and keeping them on track.

After school, I was in my room at home waiting for Mr Kensington to pick me up and drive me to the farm so that Dad and I could launch the satellites. There was a knock at the door, and Mum walked in.

"Benji, I've received emails from a few of the mums from your school today," Mum began. "When I told you that you had to stay at school if you wanted to work on the mission for Mr Crow, I didn't expect you to shut down lessons and put the entire school to work."

"I didn't either," I said. "But it's how things worked out. If we can pull it off, Mr Crow will give new computers to the entire school district."

"I don't know how you do it," she said.

"I keep telling you," I said.

"Oh right," she said. "You're a superhero."

"I'm superhero-ish," I said.

I heard Mr Kensington honk the car horn outside. "I've got to go. Dad and Mr Crow are waiting for me at the farm. We're launching the satellites tonight."

"Remember, you have school in the morning. Don't stay up too late."

I grabbed my bag and ran out to the car. Kensington opened the door, and I jumped in.

Mr Crow was waiting with Dad when I arrived. We all walked into the hangar. Dad had already attached the satellite to the spaceship. It looked a lot like the ones we'd seen up in space but it was much smaller.

"It's all ready to go," Dad said.

"Well, what are we waiting for?" I asked. "Let's launch a satellite."

I piloted the ship up to the level of LEO (Lower Earth Orbit) satellites. They travel at a height of about 160 to 1,900 kilometres above the planet. We released the first satellite and then descended to get the second.

After that we travelled a bit higher to the middle-level satellites and released the second one. Finally, we lifted the third satellite to the level of high orbiting satellites. Mr Crow explained that the companies he represented controlled about two hundred of the satellites in orbit.

My plan was that all the existing satellites that Mr Crow's group controlled would receive information as usual, but that the information would also go through my new satellites. The new satellites would work like a filter. My program slowed everything down and made it easier to understand what was happening and where things were going.

Each satellite's data was tagged with a code so we could track it as it moved through the system. One of the reasons Mr Crow's company couldn't track the thief before was because of the speed of their system. It was always churning out data and didn't have the ability to slow down and look at where the data was going or where it was being controlled from.

I remotely turned on the satellites from my ship and they blinked into life.

"Can you really keep track of all this data and make sense of it?" Dad asked.

"I suppose we'll find out. It's amazing how much money is flowing invisibly right now through all these satellites. There are billions of dollars just floating in the air. I'm not surprised someone found a way to steal some of it. It looks like the data is flowing through the new satellite well. The question now is whether the thief will strike again."

We orbited all of the satellites a little longer to make sure everything was operating correctly, and then headed back to Earth. I felt like a fisherman setting out a net. Now I just needed to wait and see if I caught anything.

CHAPTER 10
The hero never sticks around

The next day the kids at school had finished programming all the satellites and entering the codes. We spent the day monitoring and looking for anything strange, but nothing happened. All the money made by the companies flowed as it was supposed to from the shops, to the satellites, to the bank accounts.

I went home that day feeling discouraged. I had involved the whole school, I'd promised Mrs Petty new computers for the whole district and I'd promised Mr Crow I'd catch the thief. The pressure was starting to really get to me by the middle of the next day. The other kids were starting to look bored, too, and I could tell Mrs Petty was nervous that the whole thing was a mistake. Then, on the third day, it happened.

All at once the money flowing from the shops to the satellites just vanished. It was as though someone was doing a magic trick – now you see it, now you don't.

"Benji, it's happening!" Mr Crow said.

"I know," I said. "It's perfect."

"What do we do?"

"Nothing, for now. Just hold on and let the program do its magic. This is exactly what I wanted to happen. My program is already slowing the data down and tracking the flow of the money. We'll know where it's going very soon."

The money kept disappearing. It would flow into the system of satellites and then disappear. As the data flowed in, the program slowed it down. Cindy broke it into chunks and sent it to the teams. The teams watched it in slow motion to see if the data flowed anywhere unexpected or if there was a gap in the flow.

At a quarter-to-three, just before school was about to finish for the day, a girl in another class shouted, "I've got it! I've got it!"

Cindy and I ran over. "What is it?" I asked.

"The satellite I'm tracking has a break in the code. A split second before the money goes into the bank a mini-program appears for a fraction of a second and sends the money to another satellite."

"This is HUGE! All we have to do now is work out who owns that satellite, and we've got our thief," I said.

I sat down and hopped onto her computer. All the satellites orbiting the world are listed in a database. The database lists the registered owner of every satellite. I almost fell off my chair when my search returned the owner's name: Sir Robert!

"I knew he had something to do with this," Mr Crow said.

"I'm sure you did, Mr Crow," I heard Sir Robert say from behind us. We all turned in disbelief to see him standing in the doorway.

"Interesting timing," Mr Crow said. "We were just about to call the police and have you arrested."

"By all means, call the police, but they won't be arresting me."

"Sir Robert," I said. "You own the satellite being used to steal money from Mr Crow and his associates."

"You're right, Benji. I own the satellite, but I don't use it. I rent it to two of Mr Crow's assistants.

Isn't that right?" he said turning his attention to Mr Crow's assistants. The looks on their faces said it all.

"Why didn't you say something sooner?" I asked.

"I almost did, but then I learned that you were on the case and knew it would be only a matter of time until you caught these two." Sir Robert handed me a memory stick. "This contains all the information you'll need to have these two locked up."

Things were getting messy. I decided it was time to call the police. We had the data, and we knew where the money was going. The only thing left was to have the thieves arrested. Within minutes of making the call, the police and the FBI arrived at the school. There were sirens and flashing lights everywhere.

Mr Crow looked devastated. "This is going to be huge news and terrible publicity for my group."

"It'll be big news, but I don't think it has to be all bad for your group," I said, noticing a long line

of news vans streaming into the school car park. "When the reporters ask to talk to you, focus on the fact that you partnered with school kids to solve a complex computer problem. Talk about how the kids worked with satellites and programmed the computers to catch theives. People will love the fact that you included kids."

"You'll have to join me to explain how you kids did it," he said.

"I'm not the one you want talking to the reporters," I said, pointing to Cindy. "She is."

We explained everything to the police and gave them the data we'd collected. They arrested the two men who had been stealing from Mr Crow's companies.

Reporters gathered outside the school. Microphones stuck out in every direction. "I think we should go out and talk to them," I said.

We all went out, and they rushed over.

"Is it true your company was hacked and billions of dollars were stolen?" one reporter asked. Mr Crow looked my way and winked. "Yes, that's true, but the thieves have been caught and the bigger story is our partnership with Headmistress Petty and the children of her school," he said, waving Cindy and Mrs Petty over.

It worked out exactly as I'd expected. The reporters were more interested in the fact that a major computer company had partnered with a school to catch a hacker than the fact that the company had been robbed. Cindy explained to everyone how the school programmed and coded the satellites, and Mrs Petty talked about how Mr Crow's company had agreed to donate computers to the entire school district.

I slipped away and got into my limo.

Sir Robert was already inside. "Benji, did you really think I was a thief?" he asked.

I felt pretty awful. Sir Robert was my mentor. I looked up to him in so many ways, but I had also doubted him. "I know it sounds crazy, but for a moment I did. I'm sorry. I should have known better."

"No need for an apology. If I were in your shoes I might have suspected me, too."

"It looks like you've got a bit of a media circus on your hands," Kensington said. "These reporters are going to want to talk to you, too, you know."

"The hero never sticks around for a thank you," I said. "Besides, I think I'm late for my cape fitting!"

INVOICE NO: 1004968798

NOTICE OF PAYMENT

FROM: BENJI FRANKLIN
TO: MR CROW

Fuel for spaceship	$175,000
Satellite delivery	$200,000
Total cost for project	$4,175,000
20% Consulation fee	$200,000
PAID!	
Total amount due	$4,375,000

*2,000 computers No charge, supplied by Mr Crow (Value $2,200,000)
*Satellite Supplied by Mr Crow (Value $1,600,000)

PAYMENT DUE UPON RECEIPT

RAYMOND BEAN

Raymond Bean is a successful author of children's fiction. He writes for children who claim they don't like reading.

Raymond is a teacher with fifteen years of classroom experience. He lives with his wife and two children in New York, USA.

Glossary

access way to enter, or an approach to a place

associates partners in business or at work

atmosphere mixture of gases that surrounds a planet

hangar large building where aircraft are kept

mentor someone who teaches and gives help to a person who is less experienced

remotely from a distance

satellite spacecraft that is sent into orbit around the Earth, Moon or other object in space

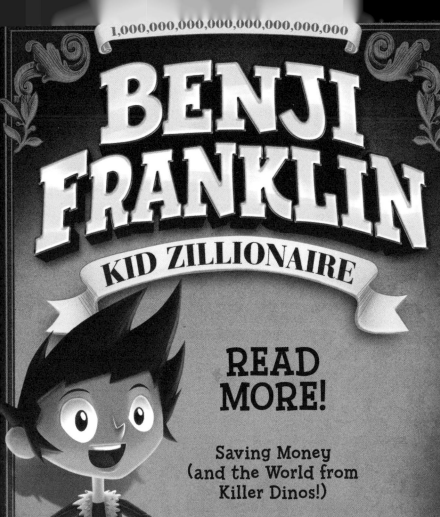

1,000,000,000,000,000,000,000,000

BENJI FRANKLIN

KID ZILLIONAIRE

READ MORE!

Saving Money
(and the World from
Killer Dinos!)

Building Wealth
(and Superpowered
Rockets!)

Buying Stocks
(and Solid Gold Submarines!)